E
Pou   Poulet, Virginia
         Blue Bug goes to Paris

DATE DUE			
DE 1 4 '87	FE 20 '90	JY 16 '92	AP 15
MR 4 '88	MR 17 '90	AUG 6 '92	SE 18
MR 24 '88	AP 21 '90	NO 2 '93	23
OC 20 '88	Y 17 '90	FEB 29 '94	JE 24
NO 3 '88	JY 31 '90	JUL 6 '94	
NO 11 '88	AG 16 '90	JL 21 '94	
JA 13 '89	MR 6 '91	FEB 13 '97	
JE 14 '89	MY 7 '91	JL 07 '97	
JY 11 '89	MY 30 '91	JL 2	
NO 14 '89	JY 25 '91	SEP 02	
FE 1	FE 11 '92	JE 27 '02	
	MY 28 '92	SE 12 '05	

MEDIALOG
Alexandria, Ky 41001

BLUE BUG GOES TO PARIS

By Virginia Poulet

Illustrated by Peggy Perry Anderson

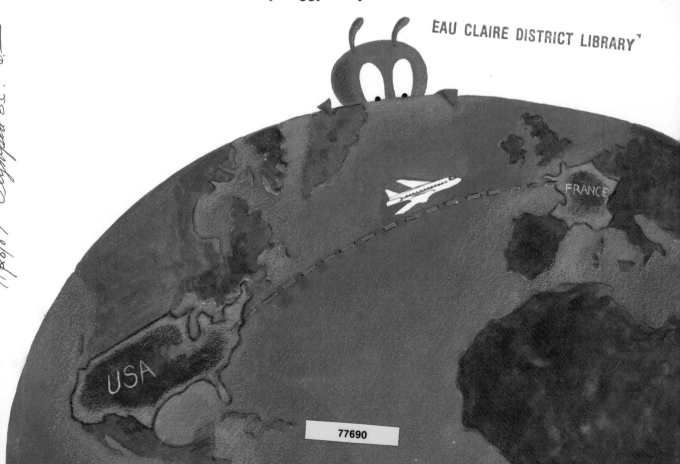

Pour Didier, Christophe, Catherine
et ma très belle belle-mère, Geneviève!

Virginia Poulet has had several opportunities to visit France. Having very much enjoyed her stays there, she wanted to share some experiences with beginning readers, to perhaps spark their interest in another culture and in a country whose people, more than 100 years ago, offered a very special gift — the Statue of Liberty — to the United States of America.

Photo credits:
United Press International
32 (bottom)
The Bettmann Archive
32 (top)
Christophe Poulet
16, 17

Library of Congress Cataloging-in-Publication Data

Poulet, Virginia.
  Blue Bug goes to Paris.

  (Blue Bug books/Virginia Poulet)
  Summary: Blue Bug goes to Paris, where he sees the sights and buys postcards and souvenirs.
    1. Paris (France)—Fiction] I. Title. II. Series: Poulet, Virginia. Blue Bug books.
PZ7.P86Bg 1986   [E]   85-31390
ISBN 0-516-03480-4

In Paris, France,

Blue Bug ate breakfast,

paid the bill, and

took the subway

to visit museums

and see famous places.

14

He saved stamps

and photographs.

The
EIFFEL
TOWER

LA TOUR
EIFFEL

After a cookie, a pastry,

NAPOLÉONS
2F 50

GÂTEAU
AU
CHOCOLA
3F

MADELEINES
12 F LA
DOUZAINE

TARTELETTES
AUX
CERISES
3F75

4F 10
ÉCLAIRS
AU
CHOCOLAT

19

CHOCOLAT

BONBONS
VARIÉS

BONBONS
A L'ORANG
25 F LE KI

20

and a candy, Blue Bug

tasted each cheese.

He visited a park

LES TUILERIES

and fed the pigeons.

Then he bought gifts and

29

postcards, and

COLONNE MORRIS

LA PLACE DE LA CONCORDE

SEINE ET LES BOUQUINISTES

31

wrote home.

PARIS 1884

The statue of Liberty before being sent to the U.S.A.

La statue de la Liberté avant son départ aux U.S.A.

I will be home soon. ♡ BLUE BUG
P.S. This is my favorite postcard